This edition published by Parragon Books Ltd in 2014

Parragon Books Ltd
Chartist House
15–17 Trim Street
Bath BA1 1HA, UK
www.parragon.com

ISBN 978-1-4723-3628-6

Printed in China

Sleeping Beauty

Bath • New York • Singapore • Hong Kong • Cologne • Delhi
Melbourne • Amsterdam • Johannesburg • Shenzhen

Long ago, in a far away land, there lived a king and queen who held a great feast to celebrate the birth of their baby daughter, Aurora.

The king of a nearby country, and his young son, Phillip, were guests at the feast.

The two kings made plans for Phillip and Aurora to marry on the princess's sixteenth birthday.

Also at the celebrations were the princess's three fairy godmothers – Flora, Fauna and Merryweather. Each of them brought a special gift for the little princess.

First, Flora waved a magic wand over the baby's cradle and said, "I give you the gift of beauty."

Then Fauna waved her wand and said, "I give you the gift of song."

Finally, Merryweather fluttered over the cradle. She raised her wand and....

Suddenly, there was a crack of thunder. Maleficent, the wicked fairy, stormed in. She was furious that she had not been invited to the celebrations.

Stroking her pet raven, Maleficent glared at the baby princess. "I also have a gift for you," she hissed. "Before the sun sets on your sixteenth birthday, you will prick your finger on the spindle of a spinning wheel and die!"

Maleficent threw back her head and laughed wickedly. Then, she disappeared in a cloud of purple smoke.

Merryweather gave a gentle cough. "I still have my gift for the princess," she reminded the horrified King and Queen.

She went over to the sleeping baby and whispered, "When the spindle pricks your finger, you will not die. Instead, you will fall into an enchanted sleep. From this slumber you shall wake when true love's kiss the spell shall break."

The King was still worried about his daughter's safety. He ordered every spinning wheel in the kingdom to be burned. Then, he and the Queen sadly agreed to the fairy godmothers' plan to protect Aurora until her sixteenth birthday had passed....

Flora, Fauna and Merryweather renamed the princess Briar Rose. They took her away to a little cottage in the woods. There, the fairies put away their magic wands. They disguised themselves as peasant women so that Maleficent wouldn't be able to find them.

11

As the years passed, Maleficent kept searching for the princess – but she never found her.

As the princess's sixteenth birthday drew nearer, Maleficent sent her trusted pet raven to try and find her. It was Maleficent's last chance....

The morning of Briar Rose's
birthday came. The three fairies sent her to
collect berries so they could prepare some
birthday surprises.

After gathering the berries, Briar Rose rested in the woodland glade. She sang about falling in love with a handsome prince.

Her friends, the animals and birds, found a cloak, a hat and a pair of boots. They dressed up as a make-believe prince. Briar Rose joined in their game, dancing and singing with them.

The clothes belonged to Prince Phillip, who after a long ride was resting in the woods with his horse.

Phillip was enchanted by the beautiful voice coming through the trees and went to find the singer.

14

As soon as they met, Briar Rose and the handsome stranger fell in love. They felt sure they had met before – once upon a dream.

When it was time for Briar Rose to leave, they arranged to meet that evening at the cottage in the woods.

Meanwhile, the three fairies were in a terrible muddle! Fauna had baked a birthday cake. But the mixture was too runny and the cake wouldn't stand up!

Flora and Merryweather had made a special gown for Briar Rose. But it was a very funny shape.

"It's no use," said Merryweather. "We need to use magic to sort this out. I'll fetch the wands."

Before they dared to use their wands, the fairies blocked up every gap in the cottage. They had to stop any magic dust escaping and alerting Maleficent to their hideaway. But they forgot the chimney!

It was so wonderful to be able to use magic again! Flora waved her wand and a beautiful pink gown appeared. Then Merryweather waved her wand and changed the gown to blue. Flora changed it back to pink. All the time, magic dust was escaping from the chimney.

Maleficent's raven was searching nearby. He saw the magic dust and decided to investigate.

By the time Briar Rose returned to the cottage, the presents were all ready. She thanked her fairy godmothers for the beautiful new gown and the delicious cake.

"This is the happiest day of my life," she said.

Then she began to tell them about the handsome stranger she had met in the woods. She planned to meet him that very evening. "It's time we told Briar Rose the truth," said Fauna. Up on the chimney, Maleficent's raven smiled.

So, Briar Rose discovered that she was really a princess and would soon have to marry Prince Phillip.

"Today you must return to the palace and start your new life," said Flora.

Briar Rose was heartbroken. She didn't want to marry the prince. She had fallen in love with the handsome stranger she had met in the woods.

By now, the raven had heard enough. He flapped his wings and flew away to tell his mistress that the search for Princess Aurora was finally over.

As soon as darkness fell, the fairy godmothers led Briar Rose through the forest to the palace. They had no idea that Maleficent was already there. Lying in wait for them....

At the palace, the fairy godmothers left Aurora in a quiet room to rest. Suddenly, a strange glowing light appeared. Aurora followed it in a trance-like state. It led her up a winding staircase to an attic room. Inside the room was Maleficent waiting by a spinning wheel.

Maleficent urged the princess to touch the spinning wheel. Aurora reached out. She pricked her finger on the spindle and fell to the floor.

As soon as the fairy godmothers found Aurora lying by the spinning wheel, they cast a sleeping spell over the entire palace.

Luckily, the fairies had discovered that Prince Phillip was the stranger with whom Briar Rose had fallen in love. Only his kiss could wake her!

So, while everyone was asleep, the fairies thought of a plan. They would return to the cottage, find Phillip and bring him back to the palace.

But they were too late! Maleficent and her soldiers had trapped the prince at the cottage and had captured him.

Maleficent took Phillip back to her castle where she threw him into her deepest dungeon. She fastened him to the wall with heavy chains and left him there to die.

When the fairies didn't find Phillip at the cottage, they guessed Maleficent may have captured him. They quickly made their way to her castle.

As soon as it was safe, the fairies magically appeared in the dungeon and freed the prince. They waved their wands and armed him with a magic shield of virtue and sword of truth.

Then, the prince galloped off to the palace to rescue the princess....

When Maleficent discovered that the prince had escaped, she roared with rage. She cast a spell and surrounded the palace with a forest of thorns.

But Phillip was able to cut his way through with his magic sword.

Suddenly, a huge and terrible black dragon appeared over him.

The dragon laughed wickedly – it was Maleficent!

Phillip held up his magic shield so that the dragon's scorching flames could not touch him.

The battle had begun! The dragon soared into the air and swooped down towards Phillip.

The prince hurled his magic sword at the dragon. The beast crashed to the ground – Maleficent was dead!

Prince Phillip raced towards the palace. He quickly found the room where the sleeping beauty lay. As he gently kissed her, she opened her eyes – the spell was broken! The fairy godmothers' spell was broken too. All round the palace, people began to wake from their enchanted sleep.

That evening, a magnificent ball was held to celebrate the wedding of Phillip and Aurora. The princess, dressed in the beautiful blue gown, danced happily in the arms of her prince.

As the fairy godmothers watched over them, Flora couldn't resist turning the blue gown back to pink. But Merryweather turned it back to blue. And so it went on ... pink ... blue ... pink ... blue....